Sabrina Sue
Loves the Moon

written and illustrated by
Priscilla Burris

Ready-to-Read

Simon Spotlight

New York   London   Toronto   Sydney   New Delhi

For Christina A. Tugeau from my grateful heart,

and in loving memory of Tina Rao

SIMON SPOTLIGHT
An imprint of Simon & Schuster Children's Publishing Division
1230 Avenue of the Americas, New York, New York 10020
This Simon Spotlight edition December 2023
Copyright © 2023 by Priscilla Burris
All rights reserved, including the right of reproduction in whole
or in part in any form.
SIMON SPOTLIGHT, READY-TO-READ, and colophon are registered
trademarks of Simon & Schuster, Inc.
For information about special discounts for bulk purchases, please contact
Simon & Schuster Special Sales at 1-866-506-1949
or business@simonandschuster.com.
Manufactured in the United States of America 1123 LAK
2 4 6 8 10 9 7 5 3 1
CIP data for this book is available from the Library of Congress.
ISBN 978-1-6659-4390-1 (hc)
ISBN 978-1-6659-4389-5 (pbk)
ISBN 978-1-6659-4391-8 (ebook)

Sabrina Sue lived on a farm.
One night she saw the moon
and the stars.

I want to go to the moon,
she thought.

She dreamed about the moon at night.

She told her farm friends about her plans.

Sabrina Sue liked being safe, but she also wanted an adventure.

Should I stay or go?

Sabrina Sue learned about the moon.

She bounced onto Farmer Martha's truck.

She huddled down under the night sky.

She went up, down,
and around and around.

She wiggled and wobbled to the ground.

She skipped all the way to the rocket.

She was ready for her trip to the moon!

10, 9, 8, 7, 6, 5, 4, 3, 2, 1 . . .
BLASTOFF!

Look! Our Earth!

Outer space is so big!

Time to land on the moon.

Goodbye, moon!

Sabrina Sue loved being back on the farm. But she knew she would visit the moon again someday!